Crossing Midnight

a map of midnight

Mike Carey
WRITER

Jim Fern
Eric Nguyen
PENCILLERS

Mark Pennington
Eric Nguyen
INKERS

José Villarrubia
COLORIST

Todd Klein
LETTERER

J.H. Williams III
ORIGINAL SERIES
COVERS

CROSSING MIDNIGHT created by
Mike Carey and **Jim Fern**

Cover illustration by J. H. Williams III
Logo design by Glenn Parsons of Astrolux Design
Publication design by Amelia Grohman

CROSSING MIDNIGHT:
A MAP OF MIDNIGHT
Published by DC Comics. Cover, afterword and
compilation copyright © 2008 DC Comics.
All Rights Reserved.
Originally published in single magazine form
as CROSSING MIDNIGHT 6-12.
Copyright © 2007 Mike Carey and Jim Fern.
All Rights Reserved.

DC Comics, 1700 Broadway, New York, NY 10019
A Warner Bros. Entertainment Company.
Printed in Canada. First Printing.
ISBN: 978-1-4012-1645-0

CONTENTS

A Map of Midnight 6

Bedtime Stories 98

Afterword 167

By Mike Carey

A Map of Midnight

Written by Mike Carey   Pencils by Jim Fern   Inks by Mark Pennington

chapter one

TOO **EARLY** TO BE AWAKE. MY HEAD STILL FULL OF SLEEP.

MY MOUTH TASTING LIKE **RUST**.

KEEP UP, HASHARITO. YOU HAVE **DUTIES** TO PERFORM.

WHAT DUTIES, KISHIMO-JIN?

THAT'S WHAT WE HAVE TO FIND OUT. YOU HAD A **DREAM** LAST NIGHT.

DESCRIBE IT TO ME.

I **LOCK** THE WORDS BEHIND CLENCHED TEETH.

THERE'S SO LITTLE THAT'S MINE. I DON'T **WANT** TO GIVE IT UP TO HER.

BUT IT'S NO **SURPRISE** TO FIND THAT SHE'S TAKEN IT ALREADY.

YOU DREAMED OF A **CHILD** WHO LIVED IN A CITY FAR FROM HERE.

A CHILD A LITTLE LIKE **YOU,** IN SOME TRIVIAL WAYS.

"SHE WAS CLIMBING A **STAIRCASE** IN A TOWER."

"A PLACE WHERE SHE WAS **FORBIDDEN** TO GO, SO HER HEART WAS FULL OF **EXCITEMENT.**"

THERE WERE **TWO** OF THEM.

A BOY AND A GIRL.

NO, YOU'RE **MISTAKEN.** SHE WAS ALONE.

"AND SHE CAME **OUT** AT LAST, ONTO THE ROOF OF THE TOWER."

"SO HIGH UP THAT THE **AIR** TASTED DIFFERENT AND THE SOUNDS FROM BELOW BLENDED INTO **MUSIC.**"

"SHE WENT UP THERE ONLY TO **LOOK,** BUT ONCE SHE WAS THERE, SHE **WONDERED.**

"IF **KNIVES** COULDN'T CUT HER, THEN PERHAPS **NOTHING** COULD HARM HER. PERHAPS SHE COULD JUMP FROM THE TOWER AND THE **WINDS** WOULD HOLD HER UP...

"BUT SHE PULLED **BACK,** WISELY, FROM THE TEST.

"DECIDING THAT A **SMALLER** TOWER MIGHT BE BEST--AND ANOTHER **TIME.**"

THE--THE **BOY** PULLED HER BACK. HE DIDN'T KNOW WHAT SHE WAS THINKING, BUT HE WAS **AFRAID** FOR HER.

BECAUSE SHE WAS TOO CLOSE TO THE **EDGE.**

THERE **WAS** NO BOY. NOW ATTEND TO ME, HASHARITO. THIS IS THE ROOM OF **TOOLS.**

WE WON'T KNOW WHAT YOUR **TASKS** ARE TO BE UNTIL YOUR TOOLS **CLAIM** YOU.

YOU MEAN, UNTIL **I** CLAIM MY--   OH!

IT'S A LITTLE FRIGHTENING AT FIRST. THERE ARE SO *MANY* OF THEM. AND THEY'RE... CURIOUS. *INTERESTED* IN ME.

THEY FLY DOWN *CLOSE* TO SEE ME BETTER.

OH, THIS IS--THIS IS *AMAZING!*

HELLO. HELLO, YOU BEAUTIFUL THING.

HMM. THEN YOU'RE TO BE A *SCRAPE-GRACE.* AS GOOD A PLACE TO START AS *ANY.*

BUT WHAT WILL I NEED *SCISSORS* FOR?

WHAT WILL I HAVE TO *CUT?*

I am not what I *seem* to be, girl-child. I am *Uso-Tsuki,* the Liar.

You can use me for a *lot* of things, but *cutting* isn't one of them.

DON'T *TALK* TO THE TOOLS. IT GIVES THEM AN EXAGGERATED SENSE OF THEIR OWN *IMPORTANCE.*

COME. NOW I HAVE TO BEGIN YOUR *TRAINING.*

OR YOU WON'T *LIVE* LONG ENOUGH TO BE USE-FUL.

THE BOY IS-- FROM MY PAST? ONE OF THE MEMORIES THAT WAS TAKEN FROM ME?

THERE IS NO BOY.

THERE NEVER WAS A BOY.

IN HERE. *QUICKLY,* NOW.

WHY DON'T *YOU* GO INSIDE FIRST, KISHIMO-JIN? AND I'LL *FOLLOW.*

STUBBORN, *SUSPICIOUS* CHILD!

THE WIND LAYS ROUGH HANDS ON HER PERSON: IT TAKES HER WHERE SHE WOULD NOT GO.

SSSSSHHHHH

THOOOOM

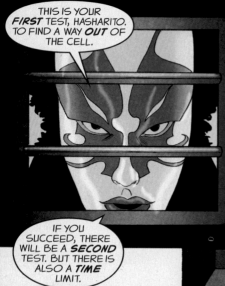

THIS IS YOUR *FIRST* TEST, HASHARITO. TO FIND A WAY *OUT* OF THE CELL.

IF YOU SUCCEED, THERE WILL BE A *SECOND* TEST. BUT THERE IS ALSO A *TIME* LIMIT.

YOU MUST COMPLETE YOUR ESCAPE BEFORE YOU *STARVE* TO DEATH.

WITH MY PRESENT SHRUNK DOWN TO A STONE CAGE, I LOOK FOR MY PAST AGAIN. BUT THERE'S NOTHING THERE.

IF I TRY TO THINK BACK FURTHER THAN LAST NIGHT, I'M THINKING INTO THROBBING GRAY HAZE.

THE SCAR TISSUE LEFT BY ARATSU'S BLADE.

I'M AN AMPUTEE.

I'M AN AMPUTEE, AND WHAT THEY'VE CUT AWAY FROM ME--

--IS MYSELF.

RINJIN-SAMA, THE *RONIN*--SHE IS COME AT LAST!

AND SHE REFUSES TO *DISARM* BEFORE ENTERING YOUR PRESENCE.

IT'S DOUBTFUL THAT SHE *COULD* DISARM, SABURO, BEING WHAT SHE IS.

SEND HER IN. AND HAVE THE GUARDS KEEP THEIR *DISTANCE* FOR THEIR OWN SAKE.

MY LORD, *NIDORU* MATERUI KITAKAMI, FORMERLY OF THE LORD *ASIROSAMIRO'S* HOUSEHOLD.

NOW OF NO *MASTER,* SINCE SHE REFUSED THE LORD *ARATSU'S* HEARTH.

LONG HAVE I DESIRED TO TALK WITH *NIDORU*--THE UNFORGIVING, THE *MASTERLESS.*

MANY AND MANY ARE THE SERVANTS I HAVE SENT TO *SEEK* HER.

CONVINCE ME THAT YOU ARE REALLY SHE.

RINJIN-SAMA, I NEED NO **SPOKESMAN** IN YOUR COURT. YOU ARE ONLY THE KING OF **SHADOWS**, AND THAT'S A **MEAGER** DOMINION. BUT, HERE--

--THESE ARE THE **SERVANTS** YOU SENT.

LET **THEM** SPEAK MY TESTIMONIAL.

NO MAN HERE IS TO **MOVE!**

IF ANY HERE LOOSES A **BOLT**, HE ANSWERS TO ME!

AND WILL YOU NOW CALL **ME** MASTER, MASTERLESS ONE?

I HAVE AN **ARMY**. I HAVE AN **ENEMY**. MY ONLY LACK IS A GENERAL.

I WILL MAKE **CAUSE** WITH YOU. I WILL FIGHT AT YOUR SIDE AGAINST **ARATSU**, THE USURPER.

BUT NO, I WILL **NOT** BE YOUR GENERAL, KUMORI-RINJIN. THAT PRECARIOUS **HONOR** BELONGS TO ANOTHER.

"YOU *KNOW* HIM, I BELIEVE.

"HIS NAME IS *KAIKOU HARA.*

"ONLY A *CHILD* NOW, BUT WITH THE PROPER INSTRUCTION--

"--I BELIEVE HE WILL BE AN ARMY ALL BY *HIMSELF.*"

I'D LIKE TO SPEAK TO DETECTIVE *YAMADA,* PLEASE.

OH, YES? AND IS DETECTIVE YAMADA *EXPECTING* YOU?

HE--NO. I DON'T THINK SO.

SIT DOWN OVER *THERE.* I'LL TELL HIM YOU'RE HERE, BUT YOU'LL HAVE TO *WAIT* UNTIL HE'S FREE.

IT COULD TAKE SOME *TIME.*

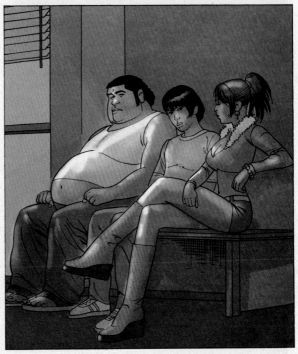

TIME PASSES.

OR *DOESN'T* PASS. I DON'T HAVE ANY WAY OF *KNOWING*.

BUT SHE WANTS MY *DESPAIR*, SO I WON'T GIVE IT TO HER.

Mistress Hasharito, to scrape out the *mortar* between the stones will take months. There must be *another* way.

Perhaps there's a hidden *door*, or a hole in the *floor* concealed beneath the rushes.

I'VE LOOKED *EVERYWHERE*. AND I DON'T THINK HASHARITO'S MY REAL *NAME*, USO-TSUKI.

I'M NOT JUST GOING TO *SIT* HERE AND WAIT UNTIL I'M TOO WEAK TO *MOVE*.

I applaud your spirit. But you could, if you wanted, try a *different* approach.

You could try *lying*.

LYING? TO *KISHIMO-JIN*?

Of course not. To the *world*.

The world is very *credulous*, and a good liar can usually *fool* it.

For example--look at those stone *pillars* over there.

THE
PILLARS?

Yes.

WHAT
ABOUT
THEM?

Nothing.
It's just that in this bad
light, they might not be
stone at all.

You could
almost imagine them
to be *trees.*

Seen
in the light
of a hunter's
moon.

YOU, WHOEVER YOU ARE.

YAMADA WILL SEE YOU ON THE ROOF.

MMWUH--?

I'M SORRY. HE'LL SEE ME--?

ON THE ROOF.

TAKE THE FIRE ESCAPE. IT'S THROUGH THE BACK OFFICE.

SO WE GO IN, AND THE STOREROOM IS FULL OF DEAD YAKUZA.

YEAH, RIGHT!

NO, SERIOUSLY. THIS ONE--THE ONE WITH HIS THROAT SLIT--HE'S TAK SAN SO, THE ONE THEY BROUGHT IN FROM CHINA.

I KNOW YOU CAN'T *TALK.* BUT YOU *GAVE* ME SOMETHING, YESTERDAY.

A MESSAGE. AT LEAST, I THINK YOU *MEANT* IT TO BE A MESSAGE.

IT'S ME AND MY *SISTER,* ISN'T IT? ME AND TOSHI STANDING ON EITHER SIDE OF *MIDNIGHT.*

SO WHAT DO YOU *KNOW* ABOUT US?

CAN YOU TELL ME IN--IN *GESTURES,* OR IN PICTURES?

WHAT DID YOU WANT TO *SAY* TO ME? WHAT DO YOU *KNOW?*

EVERYTHING.

23

chapter two

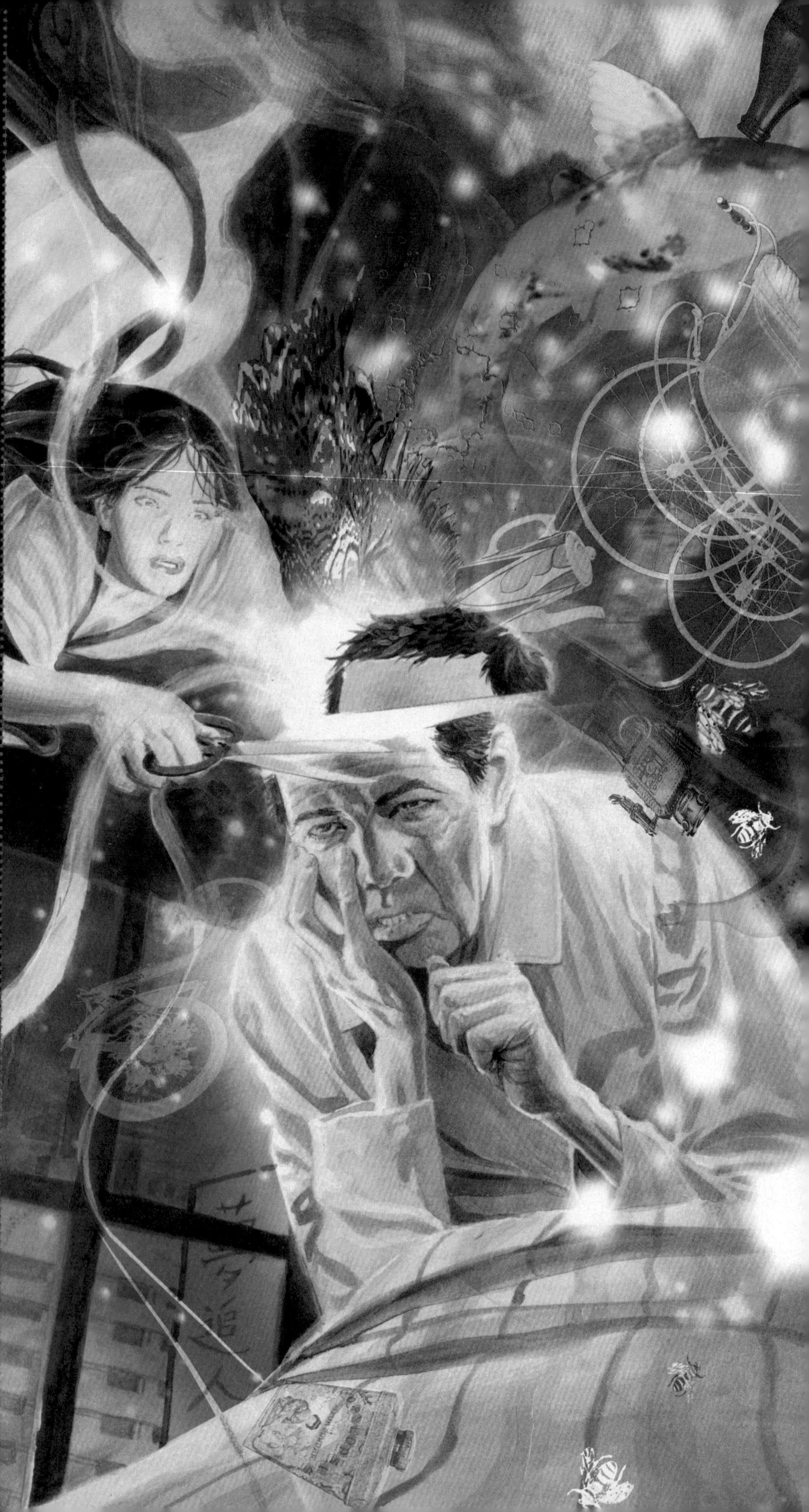

OH GOD.

I'M GOING TO DIE.

WIND TEARING THE AIR OUT OF MY MOUTH. CAN'T SCREAM.

I'M GOING TO DIE QUIETLY. AS THOUGH I DON'T MIND. AS THOUGH I ACCEPT THIS!

STUPID. STUPID TO LET THIS HAPPEN.

GINZA GRAND TOKYO PLAZA

銀座グランド

NOT EVEN KNOWING WHO I AM. NOT UNDERSTANDING ANYTHING.

NO!!

I--I CAN *FLY!* I'M FLYING!

YOUR DUTIES *REQUIRE* IT.

LIKE THE SCISSORS AND THE BOX, IT IS A *TOOL* PROVIDED BY THE LORD ARATSU.

BUT IF I'D HIT THE *GROUND,* I'D HAVE DIED. KISHIMO-JIN, YOU'D HAVE *LET* ME DIE!

CONSIDER IT ONE FINAL *TEST* OF YOUR VOCATIONAL SKILLS. NOW, FOLLOW ME...

...AND I'LL SHOW YOU WHAT A *SCRAPE-GRACE* DOES.

GOOD. A PERFECT SUBJECT. THEY'RE THE LEAST *TROUBLE* WHEN THEY'RE ASLEEP.

USO-TSUKI, EXPLAIN YOUR *PUR-POSE* TO OUR LITTLE APPRENTICE.

I was made to cut through the stuff of *thought*, mistress Hasharito.

Dip my blades into the *well* behind a man's eyes, and I can cut out the things he *dreams* about.

BUT WON'T THAT *HURT*?

No, I cut cleaner than any scalpel. There'll just be a *hole*--a thing he can't *think* about anymore.

TRY IT, HASHARITO. TOUCH HIS *FOREHEAD* AS YOU DIP THE SCISSORS.

YOU'LL SEE WHAT *PASSES* IN HIS MIND, AND YOU'LL KNOW WHEN BEST TO CUT.

Don't be afraid, mistress. I've done this *thousands* of times.

BUT NOT WITH *ME.*

Be *quick* but not hasty. Cut with a single *move-ment.*

THANK YOU, USO-TSUKI. BUT BE *QUIET* NOW.

I FEEL MY WAY. SLOWLY. EXPECTING--RESISTANCE.

BUT IT'S LIKE DIPPING YOUR HAND INTO A POND.

AND FINDING THAT IT'S FULL OF SHARKS.

USO-TSUKI **STIRS** IN MY HAND.

SLIDES HER BLADES APART, READY TO **BITE**.

IT'S SO EASY.

IT'S SO **EASY.**

GOOD. STORE THE THINGS YOU COLLECT IN THE BOX YOU WERE GIVEN. YOU'LL FIND IT MORE **CAPACIOUS** THAN IT LOOKS.

WHEN YOU'RE DONE, YOU WILL RETURN TO THE PALACE AND TAKE THE BOX TO THE **CASTELLAN.**

H-HOW DO I DO THAT?

I DON'T KNOW THE-- **OH!**

THANK YOU, BOX.

USE THIS KEY. WHEN YOU TOUCH IT AND CONCENTRATE, THE DOOR IT FITS WILL APPEAR TO YOU.

LOOK PARTICULARLY FOR DREAMS OF **DRAGONS** AND OF **SHADOWS.** AND SHOULD YOU MEET A SERVANT OF THE **GREATER** POWERS, BE POLITE AND DEFERENTIAL.

LORD ARATSU HAS **ONE** WAR ON HIS HANDS ALREADY.

"HE DOESN'T NEED *ANOTHER*."

AAAAA!

NO NO NO NO NO!

MIYA! MIYA-TYAN! IT'S ALL RIGHT, I'M HERE.

OH! OH, YASUO!

YOU'RE FINE. YOU'RE *FINE*.

NO, I'M NOT. LOOK AT MY SKIN. ALL THE *LINES* ACROSS IT. I-- I LOOK LIKE A JIG-SAW PUZZLE!

YASUO, WHERE ARE THE CHILDREN? WHAT'S HAPPENED TO THE *CHILDREN*?

I--I DON'T KNOW. KAI WAS HERE UNTIL A LITTLE WHILE AGO.

I SUPPOSE HE WENT TO TELL TOSHI ABOUT YOUR-- ACCIDENT.

THEN *CALL* THEM. MAKE SURE THEY'RE ALL RIGHT.

OF COURSE THEY'RE ALL RIGHT. THE TWINS ARE ALMOST *GROWN UP* NOW, MIYA-TYAN.

THEY *KNOW* NOT TO PLAY IN TRAFFIC.

"HAPPINESS, THEN. PARADISE, THEN. GLORY, THEN.

"WHEN I LIVED IN **REALM** OF KAMI-- INFINITE WORLD OF WHICH YOUR WORLD IS ONLY **ANTECHAMBER.**

"KNIFE-LORD **FAVORED** ME, UNWORTHY.

"UNDESERVING, I **BATHED** IN HIS COUNTENANCE.

"BUT TWO CENTURIES AGO, **NEW** BLADE FORGED.

"MASTER REQUESTED. DEMANDED.

"DECREED-- PERFECTION!

"BY FIRE, WATER, THIS BLADE **ANNEALED** FOR NINE DAYS.

"WORK. LABOR. BEAT. TEST. REFINE.

"MASTER NAMED EXQUISITE WEAPON **ARA TSU.**

"WITHOUT BLEMISH."

"IN SWORD-COURT, ALL BLADES WALKED AS MEN OR WOMEN.

"AND ALL SERVED SWORD-KING. JOYOUSLY. UNSELFISHLY.

"ARATSU CREATED TO BE *GREATEST* OF ALL.

"FIRST, PREEMINENT EMISSARY. GRACIOUS AMBASSADOR.

"SUCH--JOKE! TERRIBLE, *PAINFUL* IRONY!

"SO IDYLL ENDED. *END* BEGAN. DISGRACE.

"BETRAYAL.

"EXILE."

I MUST HAVE HAD A LIFE *BEFORE* THIS. I MUST HAVE BEEN BORN SOMEWHERE. GROWN UP SOMEWHERE.

BUT WHATEVER THAT OLD LIFE *CONTAINED,* AND WHEREVER I LIVED IT--

--I'M SURE I'VE NEVER DONE ANYTHING LIKE *THIS* BEFORE.

USO-TSUKI, IT'S SO *BEAUTIFUL!* IT MUST BE THE BIG-GEST CITY IN THE *WORLD!*

It's *ONE* of them, mistress. But we're here to work.

And the task that's before us will *fill* the night.

I KNOW. AND WE *WILL* WORK. BUT THIS IS ALL SO NEW!

THIS PLACE, AND BEING ABLE TO *FLY.* IT WON'T HURT JUST TO *EXPLORE* A LITTLE.

Will it *not?*

NO. WE'LL JUST WORK *TWICE* AS HARD LATER.

You are my *mistress,* and I bow my head.

Forgive me, mistress, but the night wears on.

ALL RIGHT, USO-TSUKI, ALL RIGHT. WE'LL COLLECT SOME **DREAMS** NOW.

AND THEN WHEN THE **MOON** IS UP WE'LL FLY SOME MORE. PERHAPS WE CAN--

...

*At the risk of **offending** you, I remind you again of the lengthy **duties** we still have to perform.*

A BOY MY OWN AGE. BUT WHAT'S HE **DOING?**

AND WHO DOES HE REMIND ME OF? I **KNEW** A BOY ONCE.

I **GROPE** FOR THE THOUGHT--

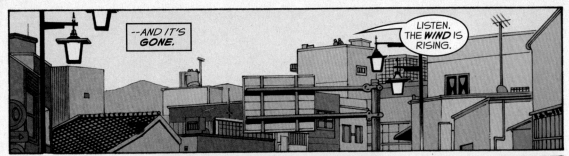

--AND IT'S GONE.

LISTEN. THE WIND IS RISING.

I DIDN'T COME HERE FOR A WEATHER FORECAST.

I SUPPOSE I HAVE TO BELIEVE WHAT YOU'RE SAYING, BUT NONE OF IT ANSWERS MY QUESTION.

I ASKED HOW YOU KNEW ABOUT ME AND TOSHI. AND YOU STILL HAVEN'T TOLD ME ANYTHING ABOUT THAT.

YOU BELONGED TO MY MASTER.

AND SO, AFTER BETRAYING HIM, FALSE LORD ARATSU INHERITED YOU.

BELONGED? BELONGED TO HIM? WHAT DOES THAT MEAN? TELL ME!

SIT DOWN. AVOID EXCESSIVE EMOTION.

TELL ME!

MY LORD TRUSTED ARATSU. BELIEVED PERFECT-SEEMING WAS SIMPLE TRUTH.

GAVE HIM SCOPE. POWER. RESPONSIBILITY.

"'OH MASTER, **BEWARE** THE FALSE ONE.

"'DO NOT LEND EAR TO HIS **POISONS.'**

"NO, NO, COULD NOT BE SAID. COULD NOT EVEN BE **THOUGHT.** BLASPHEMY!"

"IN THAT TIME, THE WOODEN SHRINES WERE MADE. MASTER SPECIFIED EXACTLY.

"THREE OF THEM. DIFFERENTLY ADORNED. EACH UNIQUE."

"THE SHRINES? LIKE THE ONE MY **GRANDMA** HAD?"

"ASIROSAMIRO **MADE** THEM? WH-WHAT FOR?"

"WAS I TO **QUESTION** MY LORD? I DID NOT KNOW WHAT FOR.

"NOW COMES **ARATSU,** BEARING A GIFT.

"'**WHAT** GIFT, MOST LOYAL OF SERVANTS?'

"' MUSIC, LORD. AND BEAUTY. AND HARMONY.

"'KISHIMO-JIN.'"

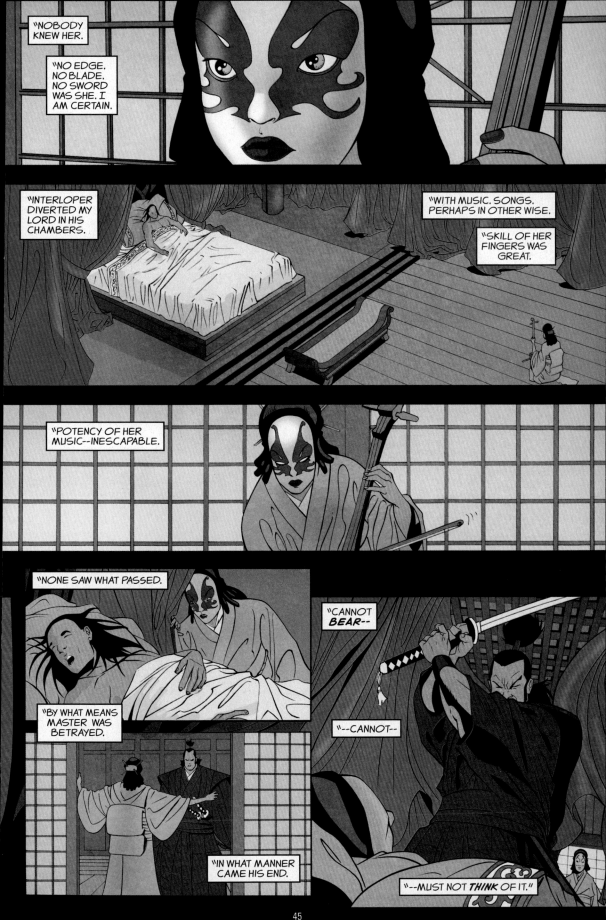

"NOBODY KNEW HER.

"NO EDGE. NO BLADE. NO SWORD WAS SHE. I AM CERTAIN.

"INTERLOPER DIVERTED MY LORD IN HIS CHAMBERS.

"WITH MUSIC. SONGS. PERHAPS IN OTHER WISE.

"SKILL OF HER FINGERS WAS GREAT.

"POTENCY OF HER MUSIC--INESCAPABLE.

"NONE SAW WHAT PASSED.

"BY WHAT MEANS MASTER WAS BETRAYED.

"IN WHAT MANNER CAME HIS END.

"CANNOT BEAR--

"--CANNOT--

"--MUST NOT THINK OF IT."

"PLANNING WAS METICULOUS. SUBORNED SOLDIERS CLOSED PALACE DOORS.

"TOLD US TO SWEAR ALLEGIANCE TO NEW LORD, OR ELSE DIE.

"NIDORU FOUND THIRD WAY. CUT HERSELF A PATH.

"ESCAPED.

"BECAME RONIN.

"I WOULD NOT SWEAR. SO FALSE ONE SUMMONED ME.

"'YOU WILL NOT GIVE ME YOUR OATH, YAMATARADA-SAN?'

"'NO, EATER OF EXCREMENT. I WILL NOT.'

"'THEN SINCE YOU GRUDGE YOUR WORDS, EACH WORD YOU SPEAK HENCEFORTH WILL TAKE A YEAR FROM YOUR LIFE.

"'GO, WITH MY BLESSING. AND PRONOUNCE YOUR OWN EPITAPH IN DUE COURSE.'"

AND SO I HAVE DONE.

WHAT IS HE *DOING?*

I don't know. But I think he serves one of the great powers. The *Chancellor,* perhaps, or the *Gleaner.*

Remember you were told not to give *offense,* mistress. Let's choose a different house.

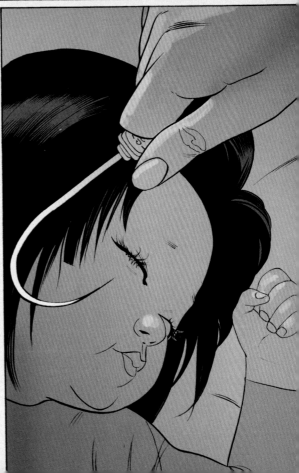

NOW RUN **AWAY**, LITTLE BOY. BEFORE YOU MAKE ME **ANGRY**.

AND WHEN YOU SEE **HER** ANGRY, YOU'LL WISH YOU'D NEVER BEEN **BORN!**

I DON'T **CARE** HOW ANGRY YOU ARE.

I'LL TELL THE **GLEANER.** I'LL TELL HER WHAT YOU DID.

It would have been better to **kill** him, mistress.

WHY? HE CAN'T **HURT** US.

No, but the **Gleaner** can. She is one of the faces of **Death.**

I'M NOT AFRAID OF THE GLEANER. I WON'T BE HERE WHEN--

OH. OH **NO!**

THE KEY--!

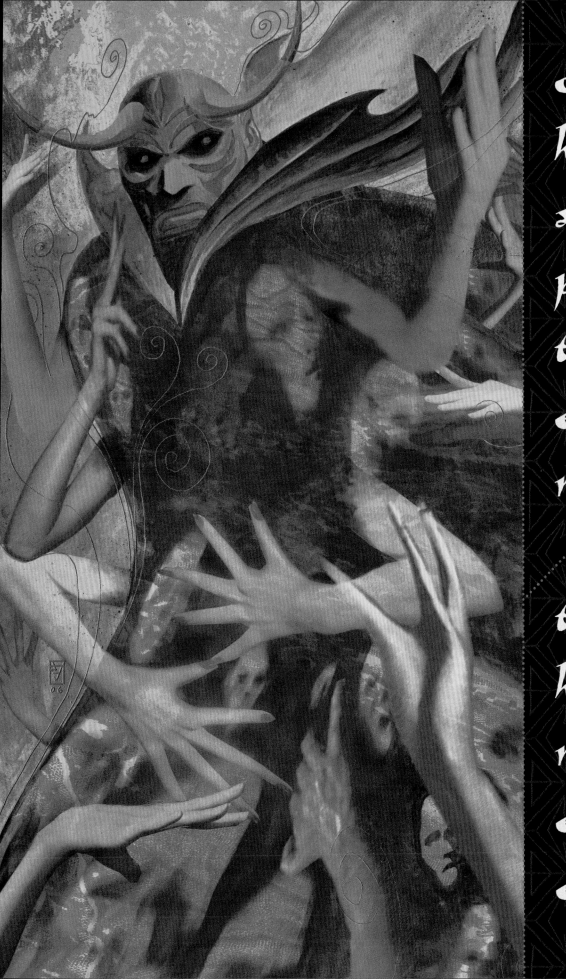

chapter three

I'VE LOST MY KEY. I'M **STRANDED.** SOMEBODY BIG AND POWERFUL AND SCARY IS **ANGRY** WITH ME.

BUT LOOK--TOKYO LIES **UNDERNEATH** ME LIKE A QUILT.

A QUILT MADE OUT OF **PEOPLE.**

SO I GUESS THAT MAKES ME A **NEEDLE.**

IN AND OUT.

UP AND DOWN.

SHARP AND PRECISE.

SO **MANY** DIFFERENT DREAMS. BUT THE INGREDIENTS ARE REALLY **SIMPLE** WHEN YOU LOOK AT THEM FROM THE OUTSIDE.

WHAT YOU **REMEMBER.**

WHAT YOU **WANT** AND CAN'T HAVE.

EWWWWW!

WHAT YOU'RE **AFRAID** OF.

...

Hasharito--

--this serves no *purpose*. We need to find a place to *hide*.

Perhaps if we can survive until *morning*, Kishimo-Jin will send someone to *find* us.

ALL RIGHT, *USO-TSUKI*. I'M COMING.

OH, LOOK AT HER! SHE'S JUST SO *BEAUTIFUL*! MAYBE SHE'S *SLEEPING* DOWNSTAIRS.

OR MAYBE THIS IS AN *OLD* PHOTO, AND SHE'S ALREADY--

This is against the *rules*, Hasharito.

NO IT ISN'T. I'M A *THIEF*, AREN'T I? THIS IS WHAT I WAS *SENT* HERE TO DO.

You were sent to steal *dreams*.

THEN I'LL DREAM ABOUT THIS *DOG*, THE NEXT TIME I SLEEP.

HAPPY NOW?

My happiness isn't at *issue*. You've already made *one* terrible mistake, and now the Gleaner--

WHO *IS* THE GLEANER?

DID YOU SAY SHE WORKS FOR *DEATH*?

She *is* Death. One of Death's aspects. Not the greatest, or the *darkest*.

But still a *kami* many, many times mightier than our master, Aratsu.

THEN I BET THERE ARE RULES FOR *HER*, TOO.

WHAT'S THE POINT OF BEING *SCARED*?

GET OUT OF THE ROAD, YOU LUNATIC!

EEEEEEEEEEEE

Hasharito, they can see you! Your cloak has failed.

I KNOW. AND I'M TRYING TO FLY, BUT I *CAN'T!* I'M BETTING I CAN'T EVEN WALK THROUGH *WALLS* ANYMORE.

IT *IS* THE GLEANER, USO-TSUKI. SHE'S WOVEN A SPELL AGAINST ME!

Then it's best we go some place where we'll attract less *attention.*

If she *comes* for you, your only hope is to hide.

ALL RIGHT.

LET'S TRY IN *HERE.*

HOUSES. MADE OF BLUE **PLASTIC**.

WHO CHOOSES TO **LIVE** LIKE THIS? IN A PLASTIC TENT IN A **PARK**?

FOR A MOMENT I CAN SEE...CARDBOARD **BOXES** BY A RIVER. MEN PEERING OUT LIKE **FOXES** FROM THEIR HOLES.

JUST A MEMORY. IT **BREAKS** LIKE A BUBBLE...

HEY, CIRCUS GIRL!

YOU WANT SOME **NOODLES**? I'LL GIVE YOU A GOOD FEED IF YOU'LL **DANCE** FOR ME!

SHE'S NOT FROM THE CIRCUS. SHE'S A **KABUKI** ACTRESS.

COME ON, SAILOR MOON. JUST A LITTLE **MOUTHFUL**.

I'M NOT **HUNGRY**. GO AWAY.

SHE NEEDS **COAXING**, WAKI-SAN. ONE FOR MUMMY. ONE FOR DADDY.

I SAID--

--LEAVE ME **ALONE**!

HAHAHAHAHAHAHA!

USO-TSUKI--?

I can't **help** you, Hasharito. Not against flesh and **blood**.

My blades are too **subtle**.

61

YOU *OKAY*, PRETTY GIRL?

I--I'M FINE, THANKS. THANK YOU.

NO PROBLEM. THIS IS UENO PARK-- *MU-RU-TSU SHIGAI*. WE KEEP THE PEACE HERE.

YOU NEED SOMEWHERE TO SPEND THE NIGHT?

I--WITH *YOU*? I DON'T-- I THINK--

LISTEN TO YOU! THAT WOULD BE *NICE*, BUT I DON'T ROB CRADLES.

LADY BOSS WILL NEED TO *LOOK* AT YOU IF YOU'RE GOING TO STAY HERE, THAT'S ALL.

IT DOESN'T SOUND LIKE THAT GOOD AN *OFFER*, BUT THEY FALL IN ON EITHER *SIDE* OF ME LIKE TWO BIG TUG BOATS.

NOBODY GETS IN THEIR WAY. NOBODY CAN EVEN MEET THEIR *EYES*.

THE LADY BOSS LIVES IN A TENT LIKE A CIRCUS *BIG TOP*.

THREE TIMES BIGGER THAN ANYONE *ELSE'S*, AND SHINING LIKE A PAPER *LANTERN* ON GION MATSURI.

MIMI-SAMA, WE BROUGHT YOU--

A *NEW* GIRL. I KNOW.

BRING HER IN, STONE-FIST. BRING HER RIGHT *IN* HERE.

COME RIGHT UP CLOSE SO I CAN *LOOK* AT YOU, SWEETIE.

I HAVEN'T GOT MY *LENSES* IN TONIGHT.

THAT'S A PRETTY STRANGE OUTFIT FOR A STREET GIRL.

DID SHE NOW? THANK YOU, CUTLASS. JUST LEAVE THEM HERE.

SHE HAD *THESE,* MIMI-SAMA.

SO. YOU'VE HAD A GOOD *STARE.*

DO YOU *RECOGNIZE* ME?

NO, I DON'T. HAVE I MET YOU BEFORE?

HAVE YOU *MET* ME? OF *COURSE* YOU HAVEN'T MET ME.

I'M *MIMI OGUNO.*

ANAL VIRGINS. BUKKAKE BATH HOUSE. SADO SEX GAMES ONE, THREE AND SEVEN.

NO? TCHAH! IF YOU WERE A *BOY,* YOU'D KNOW ALL MY VITAL STATISTICS.

THIS IS QUEEN OF CUM. WHERE I LOST MY *VIRGINITY* ON-SCREEN.

IT WAS MENTIONED IN ALL THE REVIEWS. I'M *AMAZED* YOU NEVER HEARD OF IT. AH, WELL.

JUST *SPECIAL EFFECTS,* OF COURSE. I WORKED IN A BROTHEL BEFORE THAT, AND THE MADAME HAD *SOLD* MY VIRGINITY TWICE ALREADY.

THE TAKASU CLINIC PUT MY *HYMEN* BACK EVERY TIME. TURNED ME BACK INTO A BLUSHING *MAIDEN.* WHAT'S THE MATTER, *GIRL?*

N-NOTHING.

≶CLICK≶

YOU DON'T *APPROVE* OF MY CHOICE OF CAREER?

I JUST WONDERED--IF YOU WERE SO *FAMOUS*--WHY YOU'RE LIVING IN A TENT.

LOTS OF STARS FALL FROM GRACE. FALL *FAR* ENOUGH AND YOU END UP IN UENO PARK.

MU-RU-TSU SHIGAI.

THAT'S WHAT THEY *CALL* IT, YES. "THE CITY WITH NO ROOTS." SOME- ONE MUST HAVE THOUGHT THAT WAS *FUNNY,* ONCE.

BUT IT *ISN'T.*

THERE ARE THREE *THOUSAND* HOMELESS PEOPLE LIVING IN THESE TWO SQUARE MILES. AND THE POLICE LEAVE US *ALONE.*

BECAUSE WE KEEP *ORDER.* BECAUSE WE CLEAN UP AFTER OURSELVES-- METICULOUSLY. WE MAKE SURE NOBODY *EVER* GETS ROBBED OR RAPED HERE IN THE PARK.

AND WHEN THERE'S A CONCERT OR A PARADE, MU-RU-TSU SHIGAI *DISAPPEARS.* INSIDE OF AN HOUR. EVERY ONE OF THESE TENTS CAN BE PACKED ONTO A RAILWAY STATION *HANDCART.*

"WE"?

THERE'S A *MAN-BOSS,* TOO. TIKOTO MUGI. HE USED TO BE *YAKUZA,* UNTIL HE DID TWENTY-SEVEN YEARS IN *KAYABI* JAIL.

HE'S A STERN *FATHER* TO OUR LITTLE FAMILY.

AND *YOU* WORK FOR A LIVING, TOO, DON'T YOU? YOUNG AS YOU LOOK.

THOSE ARE *MINE!*

I KNOW. I KNOW.

I DID *THAT,* TOO.

IN MY *TIME.*

YOU--YOU WERE--

A *KIZUGACHI.* A SCRAPE-GRACE. OH, YES. FOR MAYBE FIFTY, SIXTY YEARS.

YOU DON'T GROW *OLDER* WHILE YOU'RE DOING IT, SO YOU STOP COUNTING.

HOW OLD *ARE* YOU, MIMI-SAMA?

HEH! VERY *RESPECTFUL.* YOU'RE GROWING ON ME ALL THE *TIME,* DARLING.

I DON'T *KNOW* HOW OLD I AM, BUT I WAS BORN IN *MANCHURIA* JUST AFTER THE RUSSIANS TOOK IT BACK FROM US.

GASHIN SHOTAN! "PERSEVERING THROUGH *HARDSHIP."* IT WAS A TERRIBLE TIME, AND I WAS HAPPY TO GET *AWAY* FROM IT.

BUT I DIDN'T ASK WHAT THE *PRICE* WAS GOING TO BE.

AS A *WHORE* YOU LEARN TO PUT A PRICE ON EVERYTHING. BUT I WASN'T A WHORE UNTIL *AFTER-WARDS.*

AND-- THE PRICE WAS TOO *HIGH?*

YOU MIX WITH DANGEROUS *COMPANY.* YOU WADE *IN* OVER YOUR HEAD.

YOU THINK YOU CAN GET *OUT* OF ANYTHING YOU CAN GET INTO.

IF I WAS STILL IN THE BUSINESS *MYSELF,* I'D CUT HIM OUT OF THERE IN A SECOND.

WHAT DO YOU THINK, SWEETIE? ARE YOU *UP* TO IT?

USO-TSUKI, CAN WE--?

I can sever *voice* from breath, Hasharito, and light from a *lantern.*

So long as he doesn't *wake,* this will be easy.

I'LL *TRY.*

BLESS YOU, SWEETIE.

NOW, LADIES, DON'T *FRET.*

THE LITTLE GIRL IS GOING TO *CUT* ME, BUT IT WILL BE ALL RIGHT. LET HER WORK.

Hold me over her *stomach,* Hasharito.

Let me trace his *outline.*

He's big and strong. But *lazy.* He's only tied himself to her by *three* threads.

Head. Heart. Crotch. Then it's *done.*

69

BLIND **FEAR** IS ALL THAT SAVES ME. I LURCH BACK, STUMBLE--

--AND HIS SWORD **WHISPERS** OVER MY HEAD LIKE AN OBSCENE PHONE CALL.

USO-TSUKI SAVES ME FROM THE SECOND STROKE.

BUT IT **JARS** MY **ARMS** SO BADLY THAT I ALMOST DROP HER.

STUPID SCRAPE-GRACE. USED TO CUTTING **DREAMS.**

⊰UFFF!⊱

BUT **DREAMS** DON'T HIT BACK, DO THEY? **DO** THEY?

SO EAGER TO **COPE** ME, SLUTS?

I'LL SATISFY YOU **ALL** IN DUE COURSE. UNTIL THEN, JUST KNEEL WITH YOUR **HAUNCHES** IN THE AIR AND WAIT FOR ME.

AHHRRR!

Mistress! How did you *do* that?

I DON'T *KNOW.* I JUST--REMEMBERED THAT SHARP THINGS CAN'T *HURT* ME.

QUICKLY, USO-TSUKI. LET'S FINISH THIS.

THERE, MIMI-SAMA. YOU'RE *FREE.* I'M SORRY YOUR *HOUSE* GOT ALL MESSED UP.

THAT'S-- NOTHING, SWEETIE. I'M VERY-- GRATEFUL.

≶SNIK≶

YOU'RE ONE OF THE *POWERS* IN DISGUISE!

I'LL FIND OUT WHICH ONE. I'LL LEARN YOUR *NAME,* AND THEN I'LL--

WHATEVER HE WAS GOING TO SAY, THE WORDS ARE TORN INTO *TATTERS.*

THE WIND *SHRIEKS,* AND THE GUY ROPES FLICK LIKE SERPENT TONGUES.

THEN THE BLUE PLASTIC SHEETS TAKE *FLIGHT,* LIKE TERRIFIED BIRDS--

THE SKY IS FULL OF *ROPES*. LIKE THE GUY LINES OF TENTS. LIKE THE *WEBS* OF SPIDERS.

GREAT GLEANER, HAVE MERCY! HAVE *MERCY!*

ONLY THE WEB AND THE SPIDER ARE TWO PARTS OF THE SAME *MONSTER,* THAT TOWERS OVER TOKYO LIKE--

--LIKE--

--GODZILLA.

YOU HAVE *INSULTED* MY SERVANT AND *DAMAGED* MY PROPERTY.

YOU HAVE OBLIGED ME TO WALK IN THE *GREY WORLD,* ON A NIGHT WHEN I HAD OTHER ENGAGEMENTS.

IN SHORT, *TOSHI HARA,* YOU HAVE OBLIGED ME TO *NOTICE* YOU.

WHAT'S *UP* THERE, CHERRY-PIP?

YOU CAN'T *SEE* HER?

NOT A DAMN THING. AND I CAN'T *SLICE* WHAT I CAN'T SEE.

THEN STAY OUT OF IT.

THIS ISN'T YOUR FIGHT. SHE'S COME FOR ME.

MY--MY NAME IS HASHARITO. NOT WHAT YOU--*AAAH!*

NAMES ARE ONLY DRAPERIES, CHILD. DYE THEM ANY COLOR YOU LIKE--

--ONE BROKEN *STITCH* WILL UNRAVEL THEM AND SHOW THE *TRUTH.*

CAN'T LET HER SEE HOW *SCARED* I AM.

KEEP YOUR *HOOKS* OUT OF MY FACE!

MAYBE SHE CAN *SMELL* FEAR, LIKE DOGS CAN.

LIKE *DOGS?* DID THAT IDEA COME FROM THE *IMAGE* YOU WEAR AT YOUR BELT?

DOGS ARE MUCH ON YOUR *MIND.* BUT I DOUBT YOU KNOW WHY.

YOU CAN *HEAR* WHAT I'M THINKING?

I AM THE *GLEANER.* YOUR SOUL IS KERNEL, YOUR FLESH IS CHAFF.

IF THAT MEANS *YES,* THEN STOP IT. IT'S NOT *POLITE.*

AAAA!

AND THERE WE *COME* TO IT.

NAMES ARE PAINTED DAUBS. FLESH IS *HUSK* THE WIND TAKES.

BUT *ETIQUETTE* IS THE MORTAR THAT BINDS US ALL.

BUT FIRST LET ME SHOW YOU THE *GAME BOARD.*

AND THE *PIECES.*

MIMI-SAMA, ARE YOU--?

I'M ALL RIGHT, CUTLASS. I'M NOT HURT.

BUT THAT GIRL CUT OUT MY *DEMON,* AND THEN I COULDN'T DO A THING TO HELP *HER* WHEN SHE NEEDED IT.

I WAS ON MY *KNEES,* CRYING LIKE A SCHOOL-GIRL.

THE *SOULCATCHER* CALLED HER A NAME. TOSHI HARA.

THAT'S NOT WHAT SHE CALLED HERSELF.

I KNOW. ALL THE SAME, ASK AROUND. FIND OUT IF ANYBODY *KNOWS* HER.

I'M NOT GOING TO BE *HAPPY* UNTIL I'VE PAID THIS DEBT.

Nagasaki. Dejima Police Station.

YAMADA, ARE YOU SAYING EVER *WORD* OF THAT STORY COST YOU--?

YES. EVERY WORD. A *YEAR* FROM MY LIFE. AND I WAS *OLD* ALREADY.

BUT NOW YOU *KNOW* WHAT YOUR ENEMY IS. AND WHAT HE IS *NOT*.

BUT YOU DIDN'T TELL ME WHY HE TOOK MY *SISTER*.

BECAUSE OF THE *SHRINE*.

BEYOND THAT--I DO NOT KNOW.

KAIKOU HARA, I HAVE GIVEN *FREELY*. GIVEN YOU THE WORDS THAT WERE MY *LIFE*.

NOW I ASK A *BOON* IN RETURN. WILL YOU *KILL* THE USURPER, IF YOU CAN?

AFTER WHAT HE DID TO MY *MOM*? TO SEN, AND TO *TOSHI*? YES. I WILL.

THEN IF I GIVE YOU A *WEAPON*-- A GOOD ONE, OLD AND STRONG AND WELL-TEMPERED--

--WILL YOU *USE* IT? USE IT TO TAKE HIS LIFE? WILL YOU *PROMISE* ME?

SURE. I MEAN--

WHY NOT?

YES.

HOLD OUT YOUR **HAND,** THEN.

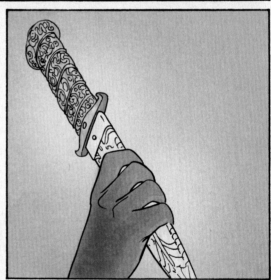

I **PROMISE,** YAMADA.

THANKS. KEEP THE *CHANGE.*

MIYA, WHAT'S THE MATTER?

NO *LIGHTS.*

WHERE ARE THE *CHILDREN,* YASUO? WHAT AREN'T YOU *TELLING* ME?

WHAT'S BEEN *HAPPENING* WHILE--WHILE I WAS SICK?

NOTHING'S BEEN HAPPENING. EVERYTHING'S FINE.

YOU'RE A VERY *BAD* LIAR.

WITH THE *CHILDREN,* EVERYTHING'S FINE. IT'S JUST-- JUST *ME.*

I'LL TELL YOU THE WHOLE STORY OVER BREAK- FAST.

NOW COME INSIDE.

THE *WIND* IS REALLY PICKING UP.

85

NOR DO I, USO-TSUKI. BUT YOU *HEARD* WHAT THE GLEANER SAID.

I THINK THIS IS THE ONLY CHANCE SHE'S GOING TO *GIVE* US.

I don't *like* this game, Hasharito.

FOLLOW IT.

AND YOU WILL *SEE.*

--AND THEN IT WAS *OBVIOUS,* HEJIRO WAS *CHEATING* THE COMPANY.

FOR THE *YAKUZA?* YOU'RE TELLING ME HE WAS A *GANGSTER?*

HE WAS BEING *USED* BY GANGSTERS, MIYA. THEY DON'T OFFER YOU MUCH OF A--

WAIT. WHAT'S THAT *SOUND?*

GUUUH!

MIYA! CHIKUSHO, MIYA, WHAT *IS* IT? WHERE DOES IT *HURT*?

MY-- GNNRRR!-- MY *CHEST*, MY--

≈HUH≈

≈HUH≈

≈HUH≈

There. That *woman*.

I SEE HER. WHO *IS* SHE?

A mortal. Do they even have *names* here in the grey world?

THE HOOK IS STUCK RIGHT THROUGH HER HEART. PERHAPS THE CHALLENGE IS TO *BREAK* IT AND SAVE HER LIFE.

That seems too easy, but as you *command*, mistress.

NO. AS I *REQUEST*.

A PERTINENT QUESTION. BUT THE *ANSWER* WILL BE LONG IN COMING. PRIZES AND *FORFEITS*, SCRAPE-GRACE. IF SHE DIES, *YOU* DIE TOO. THAT IS ALL.

NO TIME TO *ARGUE.*

IF SHE *MEANS* IT--NO TIME FOR ANYTHING.

I WONDER IF IT'S GOING TO BE LIKE THIS *EVERY* NIGHT.

Not if we mind our own *business*, perhaps.

THANK YOU, USO-TSUKI.

I ALMOST *FORGOT* THAT THIS WAS ALL MY FAULT.

IT SEEMS EASY ENOUGH, ALL THE SAME.

THE *OTHER* THREADS MOSTLY HAVE DIFFERENT TEXTURES OR THICKNESSES. YOU'VE ONLY GOT TO KEEP YOUR *EYES* OPEN.

BUT AS I GET CLOSER IN TO THE GLEANER'S *BODY*, THERE ARE MORE AND MORE OF THEM.

THOUSANDS. MILLIONS.

"I SINK THEM INTO THE *HEARTS* OF ALL THAT LIVE..."

I CAN'T *DO* THIS.

NOBODY CAN DO THIS.

⇒*NNNF!*≤

USO-TSUKI, IF I CAN FLY THROUGH *WALLS*--?

No, Hasharito. This is *spirit-weave.*

The powers and *privileges* granted to you by Lord Aratsu don't *extend* here.

NO USE.

I'M GOING TO DIE.

I'M GOING TO DIE, AND I'M GOING TO KILL SOMEONE **ELSE** AT THE SAME TIME.

BECAUSE THE ONLY THING I'M **GOOD** AT IS CUTTING THINGS, AND THIS **THREAD** CAN'T BE--

ALL RIGHT. **SHE** MADE THE RULES.

Hasharito, you see a **way?**

I SEE-- **SOMETHING.** I DON'T KNOW.

BUT I HAVE TO **TRY.**

THIS IS **STUPID.** GAMBLING EVERYTHING ON--WHAT?

AN **ACCIDENT.** SOMETHING I DID ONLY ONCE, AND THEN WITHOUT MEANING TO.

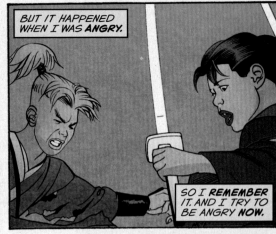

BUT IT HAPPENED WHEN I WAS **ANGRY.**

SO I **REMEMBER** IT. AND I TRY TO BE ANGRY **NOW.**

NOTHING.

I THINK ABOUT **KISHIMO-JIN,** WHO I HATE.

AND ABOUT ALL THE **HUMILIATIONS** AND THE SNEAKY, DEADLY LITTLE **TRICKS** SHE PLAYED ON ME.

STILL NOTHING COMES.

WHAT ABOUT THE MOMENT WHEN I WAS **BORN?**

IN ARATSU'S **CHAMBERS.**

MY CHEST **BURNING** WHERE HIS SWORD HAD JUST CUT AWAY MY PAST AND MY **FUTURE.**

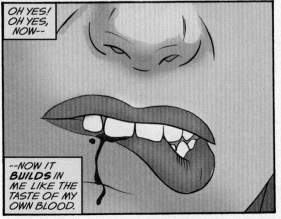

OH YES! OH YES, NOW--

--NOW IT **BUILDS** IN ME LIKE THE TASTE OF MY OWN BLOOD.

FEEDING ON **ECHOES** OF LONG-DEAD MOMENTS.

DESPERATE TO BE SPOKEN.

CLAWING ITS WAY INTO THE **WORLD--**

I SHOULD HAVE LEARNED **CAUTION** BY NOW, BUT I'M STILL SO **EXCITED** ABOUT WHAT I'VE JUST DONE.

I **RACE** IT TO THE GROUND, LIKE A **DOG** CHASING A STICK.

LIKE--

--LIKE A--

OH, SHE'S **BEAUTIFUL!** SHE'S **BEAUTIFUL!** WHERE DID SHE **COME** FROM?

HERE, GIRL!

FROM THE SMOKE OF AN INDUSTRIAL **FURNACE** BEHIND A MORTUARY IN THIS CITY. AND FROM YOUR OWN **THOUGHTS.**

FAREWELL FOR NOW, SCRAPE-GRACE. I **RETURN** YOU TO YOUR LIFE.

THE AIR RIPS **OPEN** LIKE A SOGGY PAPER BAG.

TOKYO IS THERE. IT'S **OVER.** I'VE **BEATEN** THE GLEANER, AND I HAVE A NEW **FRIEND.**

OR PERHAPS AN OLD ONE. FOR A MOMENT THAT THOUGHT MAKES ME *DIZZY.*

"*I RETURN YOU TO YOUR LIFE...*"

I HAD *ANOTHER* LIFE, ONCE. AND IT WAS CUT *AWAY* FROM ME.

BUT I CAN GET IT *BACK.*

T--TOSHI?

TOSHI!

TOSHI!! WAIT!!

I *WILL* GET IT BACK. I'LL FIND MY HOME AGAIN SOME DAY, AND I'LL GO THERE.

LOOK, USO-TSUKI. THE *SUN* IS COMING UP.

It usually *does,* mistress.

I'd read no *OMEN* in that.

WE CAN IF WE *LIKE,* CAN'T WE, SUPER-DOG?

WE CAN IF WE *LIKE.*

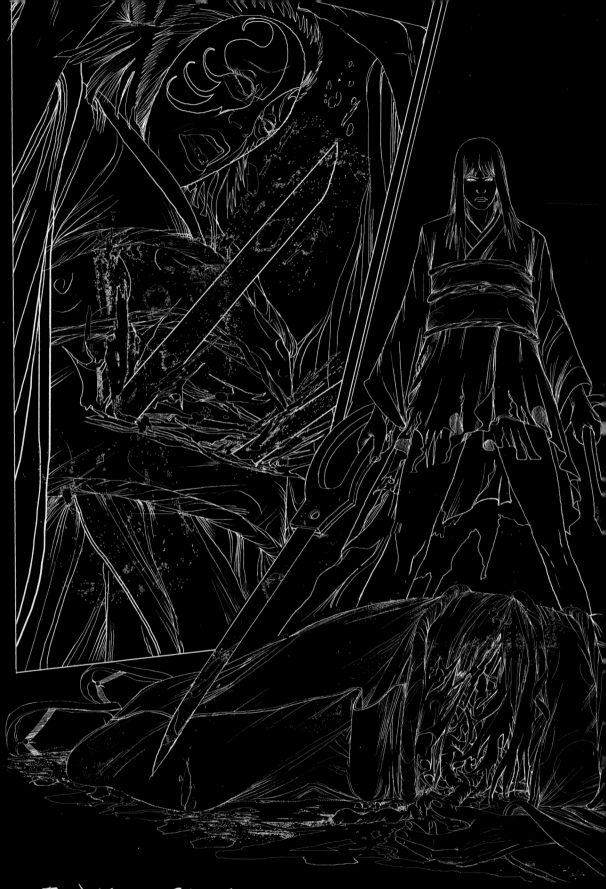

Bedtime Stories

Written by Mike Carey   Art by Eric Nguyen

I was going to say it was the *party*. But it wasn't the party.

It was the *cake*.

At Terekura Jing-Jing, where the telephones are *sexual aids*, the *enjokosai* girls gather to pick up their *dates*.

Stand around and gossip, looking even younger than their age in their super-cute *kawaii* clothes.

But today, *Loretta* and *Kitty-Ki* cut the session short.

They found some urgent pretext to send *Pink* away to the hotel room they keep on *Ihoma*.

Then when she was gone, they got *busy*, making the place look nice.

And making the bemused *masturbators* uneasy with this reminder of another *world*, another life.

Pink walked back in to *"Happy Birthday!"*, three cheers and an endless *array* of hugs and kisses.

And a *cake*.

Which bore a whimsical *decoration* in place of a candle.

How they *roared*, the rented children, at their own bad *joke*.

"Blow it out, Pink!" "*Blow* it--!" They couldn't finish the *sentence* for laughing.

But I was *weeping* as I watched. Wrenching, silent sobs, like the dry *heaves* of ague.

Until something *broke* in my heart, in my guts.

There is no *ladies'* toilet at Terekura Jing-Jing.

By special dispensation, the girls are allowed to use the *staff* toilet out in the back behind the *store* cupboards.

OH!

OH, LOOK AT YOU!

JUST *LOOK* AT YOU!

YOU'RE SO--

IT FEELS LIKE A LONG SHOT.

BUT YOU'LL TAKE A LONG SHOT WHEN IT'S THE ONLY SHOT YOU'VE GOT.

TOKYO POLICE

WHEN I SAW TOSHI OUTSIDE OUR APARTMENT, SHE WALKED THROUGH A DOORWAY IN THE AIR.

AND I SAW--

--I THOUGHT I SAW--

--THE TOKYO SKYLINE BEHIND HER AS THE DOORWAY CLOSED.

IT'S IN SO MANY MOVIES, YOU CAN'T MISTAKE IT FOR ANY- WHERE ELSE IN THE WORLD.

BUT IT LOOKS A LITTLE DIFFERENT WHEN YOU'RE LOST IN THE MIDDLE OF IT.

I CAN'T *BELIEVE* IT!

SHE CAN'T BE *DEAD*! SHE *CAN'T!*

IT MUST HAVE HAPPENED WHEN WE WERE SI-SINGING. OTHER-WISE WE WOULD'VE *HEARD.* OH, GOD!

WE COULDN'T HAVE *KNOWN,* PINK.

IT'S NOT YOUR *FAULT.* IT'S NOT *ANYONE'S* FAULT.

SHE WAS *MURDERED.* OF *COURSE* IT WAS SOMEONE'S FAULT.

ONE OF THE *MEN* THERE PROBABLY KILLED HER. YOU SHOULD HAVE STAYED AND GIVEN THE POLICE THEIR *DESCRIPTIONS.*

IT'S NOT YOUR *LIFE,* COUNTRY BOY. YOU DON'T KNOW ANYTHING ABOUT IT.

NO, YOU'RE RIGHT. I DON'T.

I DON'T UNDERSTAND *ANY* OF THIS.

DON'T THEY *HAVE* ENJOKOSAI WHERE YOU COME FROM?

DON'T YOU KNOW WHAT A *REWARD* DATE IS?

OKAY. I'M NOT *STUPID*.

YOU'RE *PROSTITUTES*, RIGHT?

WHAT??

YOU'RE NOT *STUPID*? YOU'RE WHAT HAPPENS WHEN PEOPLE GET *PAST* STUPID AND COME OUT THE OTHER SIDE.

I'M *NOT* A PROSTITUTE!! I'M A *DATE* GIRL!

OW! OKAY!

PROSTITUTES HAVE *SEX* WITH MEN FOR MONEY.

I DO... *OTHER* STUFF. MOSTLY.

AND IT'S *COMPLETELY* DIFFERENT.

OKAY. BUT I MEAN--IF YOU CAN AFFORD TO LIVE *HERE*--

WE DON'T *LIVE* HERE, COUNTRY BOY. WE JUST KEEP OUR *THINGS* HERE.

I'M GOING HOME. I CAN'T *STAND* THIS. IT'S THE WORST BIRTHDAY I'VE EVER *HAD*.

CALL ME WHEN YOU GET IN.

OKAY.

SERIOUSLY. I'LL *WORRY* ABOUT YOU IF YOU DON'T.

WELL, I *WILL*.

What is *innocence?*

Where does it *go* to, when it's lost? Stolen?

YOU'VE GOT...NO... YOU'VE GOT NO STY-Y-Y-YLE.

Or simply thrown *away?*

It gathers in the *clouds*, like rain.

OHHH! I *SAW* YOU IN--

It falls like *tears*.

MOSTLY, THE GUYS WE SEE JUST WANT TO *TOUCH* US. SMELL OUR HAIR. STUFF LIKE THAT.

BUT IF THEY *DO* ASK FOR MORE, AND IF WE WANT TO GIVE IT--WELL, THEN WE'VE GOT *THIS* PLACE TO TAKE THEM BACK TO.

AND YOU STILL LIVE WITH YOUR *PARENTS?*

AND--THEY DON'T HAVE ANY *IDEA* THAT YOU DO THIS?

MY DAD WORKS FOR *FIRST PENINSULAR.* HE ONLY COMES HOME TO SLEEP.

AND MY MOM STILL THINKS I'M *TWELVE.* SHE'D PEE HERSELF IF SHE EVEN KNEW I'D *KISSED* A BOY.

THEN... WHY?

WHY? BECAUSE I *WANT* STUFF I CAN'T AFFORD. CLOTHES. PHONES. PERFUME.

AND BECAUSE IT'S *FUN.*

FUN? YOU PICK UP MEN ON THE *STREET,* AND ONE OF YOUR BEST FRIENDS WAS JUST *MURDERED.*

NO OFFENSE, BUT--ARE YOU *CRAZY?*

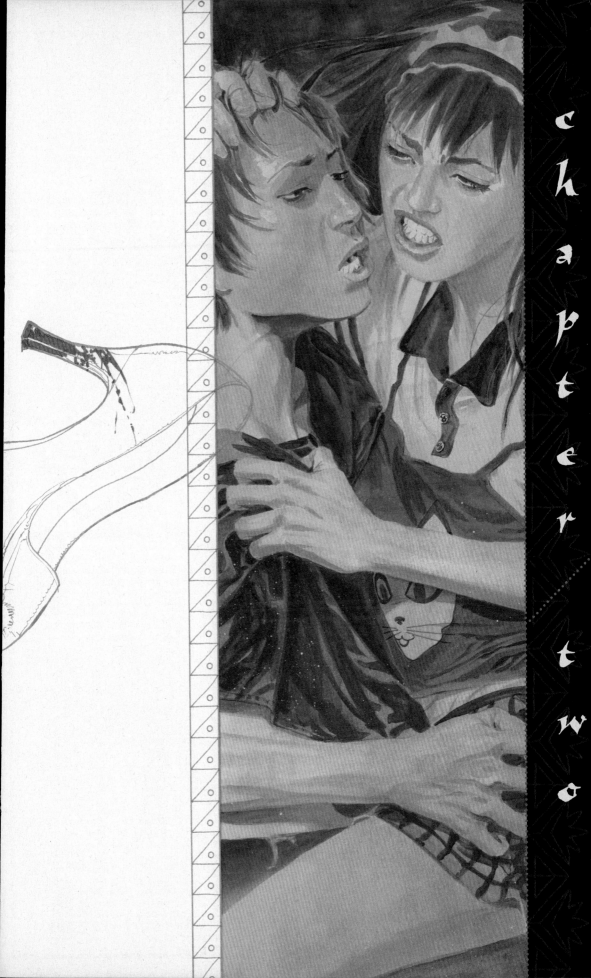

chapter two

This one's name is *Osura*, but she calls herself Bijou.

After a character in a story her *mother* told her when she was six.

A cute, furry *animal* that walked and talked.

She wears that name, and yet she *struts* in unfeasible heels.

In slit *skirts* that show the fork of her legs with each step she *makes*.

She hides her *face* beneath a mask of garish, clashing colors.

The sickening *parody* of a child courtesan.

This is what innocence has *become,* then.

An ironic *gesture.*

Adding pith and piquancy--

WH-WHO'S THERE?

--to the decadent *feast* of flesh and spirit.

Tokyo.

The Imperial Hotel.

≶HUH≶

≶HUH≶

≶HUH≶

OKAY, JUST-- SIT THERE UNTIL YOU GET YOUR *BREATH* BACK.

IT'S ALL RIGHT, LORETTA. IT'S ALL *RIGHT*.

ARE YOU *INSANE,* KAI? THAT'S PINK UP THERE, STUCK INSIDE A *MIRROR!*

HOW CAN IT BE ALL RIGHT?

AT LEAST SHE DIDN'T *DIE* LIKE KITTY-KI. MAYBE WE CAN GET HER *OUT.*

SURE WE CAN. THERE'S AN EMERGENCY-OPEN-*MIRROR* BUTTON RIGHT THERE NEXT TO THE ELEVATOR.

JUST SHUT *UP,* COUNTRY BOY, OKAY?

bip bip bip

HELLO, CANDY? THIS IS LORETTA.

LISTEN, DON'T GO TO THE *PHONE CLUB* TONIGHT. DON'T GO NEAR IT.

SOMEONE'S TRYING TO *KILL* US. SPREAD THE WORD AROUND.

YOU'RE GOING TO CALL ALL THE DATE GIRLS YOU KNOW?

YES.

CAN I *HELP?*

NO. YOU *CAN'T.*

bip bip bip

KIKU? DON'T GO TO THE CLUB TONIGHT. AND DON'T GO OUT ON A DATE.

JUST *DON'T.* I'LL TELL YOU LATER.

bip bip bip

"I TRAVEL *LIGHT*."

"AND YOU'RE JUST EXCESS *BAGGAGE*."

YOU *SENT* FOR ME, LORD ARATSU.

ONLY IN ANSWER TO YOUR OWN *REQUEST*, HASHARITO.

MY AGENDA THEREFORE WAITS UPON *YOURS*.

I FOUGHT THE *GLEANER*.

I INSULTED HER SERVANT, SO SHE *FOUND* ME. SHE SET ME A CHALLENGE.

I FOUGHT HER AND *WON*.

I WONDER WHY SHE DID NOT SIMPLY *DESTROY* YOU.

ALSO WHY YOU SEE FIT TO *BRING* THIS NEWS TO ME.

BECAUSE IT'S *IMPORTANT*.

AND BECAUSE IT SHOWS YOU WHAT I CAN *DO*. EVEN *WITHOUT* MY MEMORIES.

EVEN STUMBLING AROUND IN THE *DARK*, AS I AM NOW.

DO YOU EXPECT ME TO BE *IMPRESSED* BY SUCH A DISPLAY?

BY POWER WITHOUT *FINESSE?* BY WANTON *DISREGARD* OF GRACE AND SUBTLETY?

SOMEHOW I DON'T THINK *SUBTLETY* IS WHAT I'M GOING TO BE GOOD AT. GIVE ME MY *LIFE* BACK.

OR ELSE GIVE ME A *JOB* THAT DOESN'T INVOLVE STICKING MY HANDS IN OTHER PEOPLE'S *HEADS.*

AH. SO YOU THINK YOU'RE READY FOR *WEIGHTIER* RESPONSI-BILITIES?

YOU'D LIKE TO PROVE THAT YOU CAN BE *TRUSTED* WITH MY HONOR AND YOUR OWN PAST *LIFE?*

YES.

VERY WELL, HASHARITO. YOU'LL *HAVE* YOUR CHANCE.

I WILL *PROMOTE* YOU FROM SCRAPE-GRACE--

--TO *ASSASSIN.*

AND ICHI IS THE *FIRST* TO SNATCH A RING! OH, BUT HE'S DOWN! HE'S DOWN IN THE *MUD!*

WHAT WILL HIS *FORFEIT* BE? LET'S HAVE THOSE VOTES RIGHT NOW!

BONG CLANG

OOOOH, IT'S THE *STINK-CHAIR!* VERY UNSANITARY AND VERY SMELLY!

TRY TO KEEP YOUR *MOUTH* SHUT, ICHI-SAN!

BONG CLANGG

UMMM--HELLO, MRS. TAKUYA. WE'RE FRIENDS OF BIJ--

--OF *OSURA*. WE WERE WONDERING IF WE COULD PLEASE SEE HER.

SHE'S IN HER ROOM. DOING HER *HOMEWORK,* LIKE YOU SHOULD BE.

YOU CAN SEE HER FOR *FIVE MINUTES.* I DON'T WANT HER TO BE DISTRACTED.

BIJOU? CAN WE COME *IN?*

I JUST WANT TO--

--TO--

OH **GOD!** BWCHHHH!

STAY HERE.

WHAT? KAI, YOU CAN'T--

I JUST WANT TO GET A **CLOSER** LOOK.

YOU'RE **SICK!**

WE NEED TO KNOW HOW SHE **DIED.**

WHY?

TO SEE IF THERE'S ANY **PATTERN.**

YOU'RE WALKING IN HER **BLOOD!**

I KNOW. I'M--SORT OF **USED** TO THAT NOW.

IT DOESN'T **BOTHER** ME IF IT'S SOMEONE I DIDN'T KNOW.

I CAN'T **STAY** HERE.

IF I STAY HERE, I'M GOING TO THROW **UP.**

AND I DON'T **WANT** TO THROW UP ALL OVER MY FRIEND'S DEAD BODY.

OKAY, I'M--

YEAH. FINE. LET'S GO.

NO PRIZE! NO **PRIZE** FOR YOU BECAUSE YOU WERE SO CLUMSY!

SEE? THE BOX IS **EMPTY!** HAHA HAHAHAHA HAHA!

AT *TARIMOKU?* I DON'T GET IT.

I FOUND GOLDEN-BROWN *FUR* NEXT TO BIJOU'S BODY.

AND LACQUERED *WOOD.*

WOW! INSPECTOR NAGASAKI INVESTIGATES! YOU REALIZE TARIMOKU DOESN'T *EXIST,* RIGHT?

AND THAT IF HE *DID,* HE'D BE CUTE AND CUDDLY?

YOU SAID YOU'VE BEEN *DREAMING* ABOUT HIM.

IN YOUR DREAMS, WHAT DOES HE *DO?*

HE *CRIES.*

ABOUT WHAT?

I DON'T KNOW. I'LL *ASK* HIM NEXT TIME I'M ASLEEP. DO YOU HAVE ANY IDEA HOW *WEIRD* YOU ARE?

BUT HE'S *UNHAPPY* ABOUT SOMETHING?

WAIT! WHERE ARE YOU *GOING?*

AWAY FROM *YOU,* YOU PSYCHO.

I'M SICK OF YOU PRETENDING TO KNOW WHAT'S *HAPPENING* HERE.

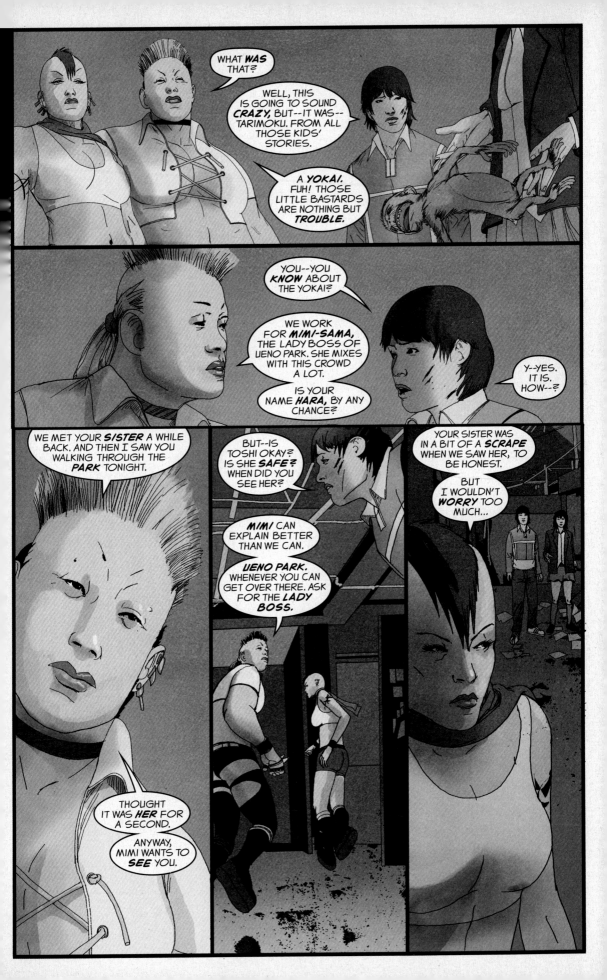

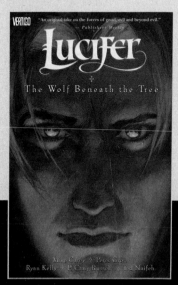

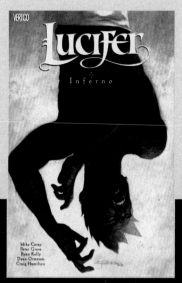

Innocence for Sale or Rent

The second story arc in this collection deals with a phenomenon which is both very difficult for Westerners to understand and hugely controversial within Japan itself: the phenomenon of *enjokosai*, which is usually translated as "reward dating" or "compensated dating." I thought it might be useful to add a few comments here about this practice and its place in Japanese culture, for the benefit of readers who may find their minds gently boggling as they read through this chapter and encounter the characters of Loretta, Kitty-Ki and Pink.

Obviously, teenage prostitution is a worldwide problem. It's not restricted to Japan, and it's not something we can ever afford to think of as "someone else's problem." But the situation in Japan has some features that aren't reproduced elsewhere, and the cultural context is different. Japanese popular culture openly eroticizes underage girls, with a large and mostly legal industry catering to a sexual fetish which in the West is more aggressively legislated against. Manga images of children in sexual poses and acts are available to buy in ordinary news outlets, and high school girls who want to engage in prostitution find a sophisticated support network already in place to help them do so.

The most important element in this support network is the *terekura*: the telephone club. In Europe and America, sex chat lines mostly advertise through magazines and websites, and the men who use them make their calls from home. In Japan, the men are more likely to go to phone clubs. Here, they can engage in sex chats with women, and, if they want to, they can masturbate while they're talking. But they can also access lists of phone numbers left at the club by girls looking for an actual meeting — and a significant proportion of these girls will be of middle school and high school age.

The resulting "reward date" may not involve actual sex. Each girl — in theory at least — can choose how far she wants to go and how much she wants to charge for it. The girls are aware that the commodity they're really offering, their unique selling point, is innocence. They typically dress in *kawaii* styles, emphasizing their youth and cuteness. The men they meet may either pay them in cash or buy them expensive gifts. The date may be a one-off or may be the start of a protracted relationship.

In some ways, this can all look a lot less malign than teenage prostitution in the West. The girls seem to have more control over the transaction, they're not owned or victimized by a pimp, and they're not sleeping rough on the streets or living in disease-ridden squats. They get to keep whatever they make (many seem motivated by a desire to buy designer clothes and accessories) and they can stop at any time — in theory, anyway. Jennifer Liddy, writing in the online magazine *Freezerbox*, remarks that when she discusses *enjokosai* with her Japanese friends and colleagues, they're very unwilling to see the girls as victims, or to attach any stigma to the men who pay for their (insert euphemistic quote marks) company.

It's difficult to get an estimate for how widespread this whole phenomenon is, but according to a Tokyo Metropolitan Authority survey of 1996, 4% of all high school girls in Tokyo admitted to having acted as paid escorts. A more recent survey across the whole of Japan, by the Congress of Parents' and Teachers' Associations, found that 25% of their teenaged sample were "regularly" involved with telephone clubs in one way or another — either just chatting or using them to set up reward dates.

I'm not making these points in order to raise any kind of moral panic or to encourage anyone to shake their heads in holier-than-thou horror at how depraved Japanese men are. Let's be blunt: I don't know about the United States, but London appears to be becoming the forced prostitution capital of the goddamned world, with up to a quarter of all girls kidnapped or coerced into sex work in Europe probably going through the UK at some point in their nightmare journey. Speaking as a Brit, I am in no position to cast the first stone here.

All I'm doing is trying to give you a sense of where Loretta and her friends are coming from. They're a product of their culture, and they're a part of something that's real and significant and ongoing — neither fantastic nor exaggerated for effect. And if they make you feel uneasy, good. They really should.

PS: In the UK, there's a charity called Eaves Housing which works to get young girls out of prostitution. In the U.S., there's a group called ECPAT with a similar but broader mission, and in Japan itself there's *Kanita Fujin No Mura*, the "Women's Village" organization. If you want to donate, they're only a Google search away.

MIKE CAREY
2007